Sleeping Beauty

A story by Charles Perrault

retold by Joy Cowley

Illustrated by So-yeong Kim

Once there lived a king and queen
who were very happy, but for one thing,
they did not have a child.

The queen prayed every day,
"Please, let me have a child."
One day she became pregnant
and she gave birth to a beautiful girl.

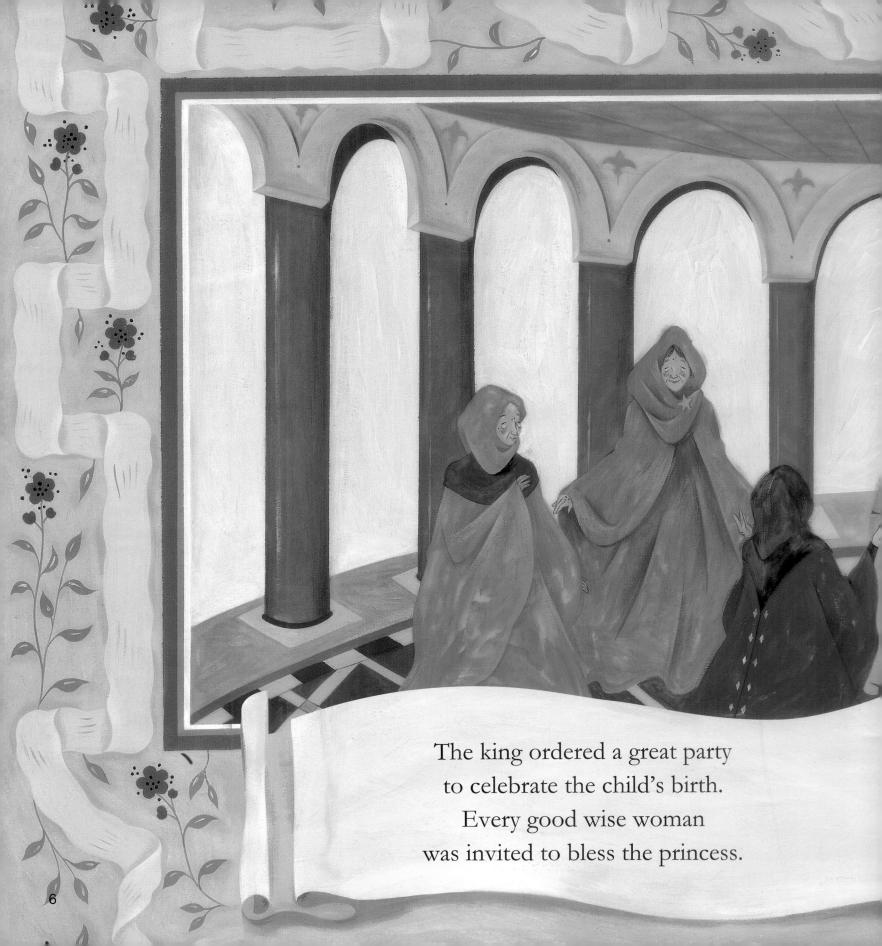

The king ordered a great party
to celebrate the child's birth.
Every good wise woman
was invited to bless the princess.

6

"She will always be beautiful."
"She will dance and sing well."
"She will be good and kind."

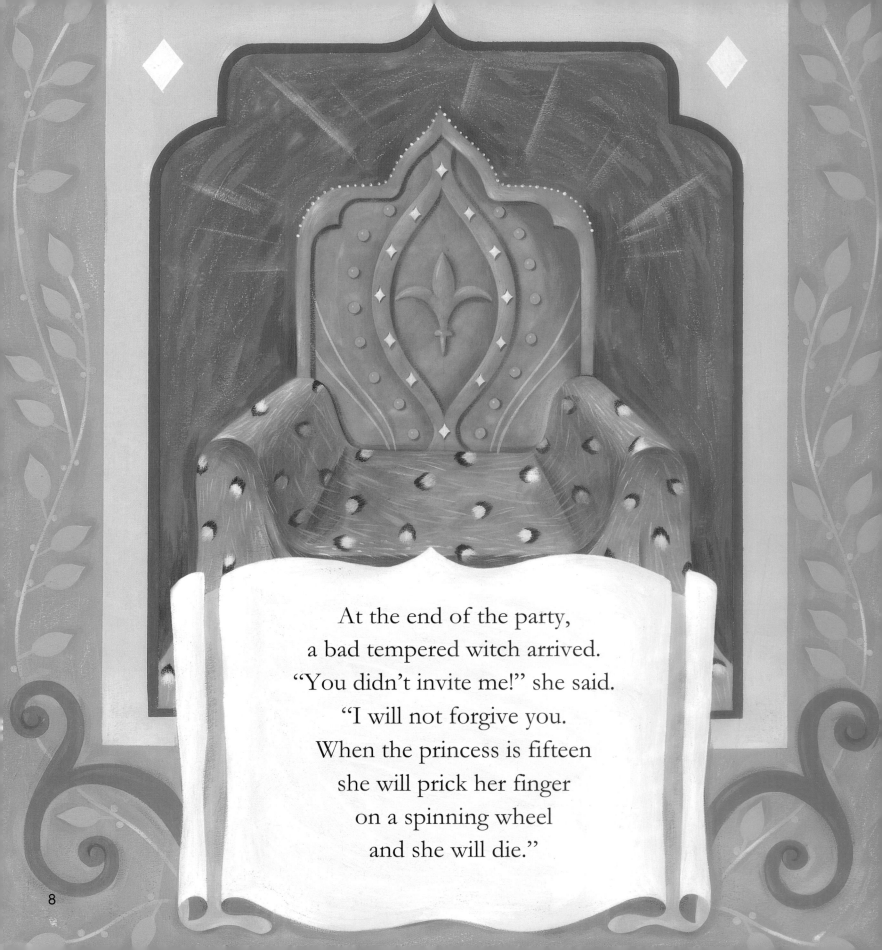

At the end of the party,
a bad tempered witch arrived.
"You didn't invite me!" she said.
"I will not forgive you.
When the princess is fifteen
she will prick her finger
on a spinning wheel
and she will die."

The witch disappeared,
leaving the king and queen
in a state of shock.

"What can we do?"
cried the queen.

A good wise woman
who had not yet blessed the baby
came forward and said, "Don't worry.
I will break the witch's evil spell.
The princess will sleep for one hundred years.
Then a prince will come and rescue her."

The king, hoping to avoid the spell,
ordered that all the spinning wheels
in the kingdom should be burned.

The princess grew up.
She was talented, beautiful,
and so kind that everybody loved her.
By the time she had her fifteenth birthday,
people had forgotten about the curse.

One day, the princess
heard a strange noise
in the tower of the castle.
"I wonder what is happening,"
she said, and she ran up the stairs.

In a small room at the top of the tower,
an old woman was spinning flax.
"Would you like to try, my dear?"
asked the woman.

The princess nodded
and sat down at the spinning wheel.

At once, the princess pricked her hand.

The old woman laughed and laughed.
"Ha ha! You can't escape from my spell!"

17

The princess sighed and

fell down in a deep sleep.

The good wise woman waved her wand
to make everyone in the castle
fall asleep with the princess.

Gently, the king and queen went to sleep
and a thorn hedge grew up around the castle.

21

One hundred years later, a prince came riding by.
He looked at the castle and wondered why
it was covered with sharp thorns.

People told him the story
of the sleeping princess.
"I will rescue her," said the prince.

The prince learned that the thorns
strangled people who went near them.
But the good wise woman
gave him a sword and a shield.
"These will protect you
from the thorn hedge," she said.

As the prince approached the castle,
the thorn hedge became more dense.
The branches wrapped around him
and he needed to hack his way through.

The evil witch saw the prince
and she turned herself into a dragon.
She rushed at the prince, breathing fire.

The prince held up his shield
to deflect the fire back on the dragon.
The evil witch turned into a fireball
and in an instant, she died.

27

The prince arrived at the top of the tower.
When he saw the princess, he was amazed
at her beauty. Gently he kissed her,
and the princess slowly woke up
from her hundred year deep sleep.

The evil spell had been broken by a kiss.

As soon as the princess woke up,
the people in the castle also woke.
How happy the king and queen were
to see their daughter alive and well.

The prince was in love with the princess and asked the king if he could marry her. "With my blessing!" said the king.

Everyone in the kingdom
celebrated the wedding,
and the good wise woman
wished them all happiness.

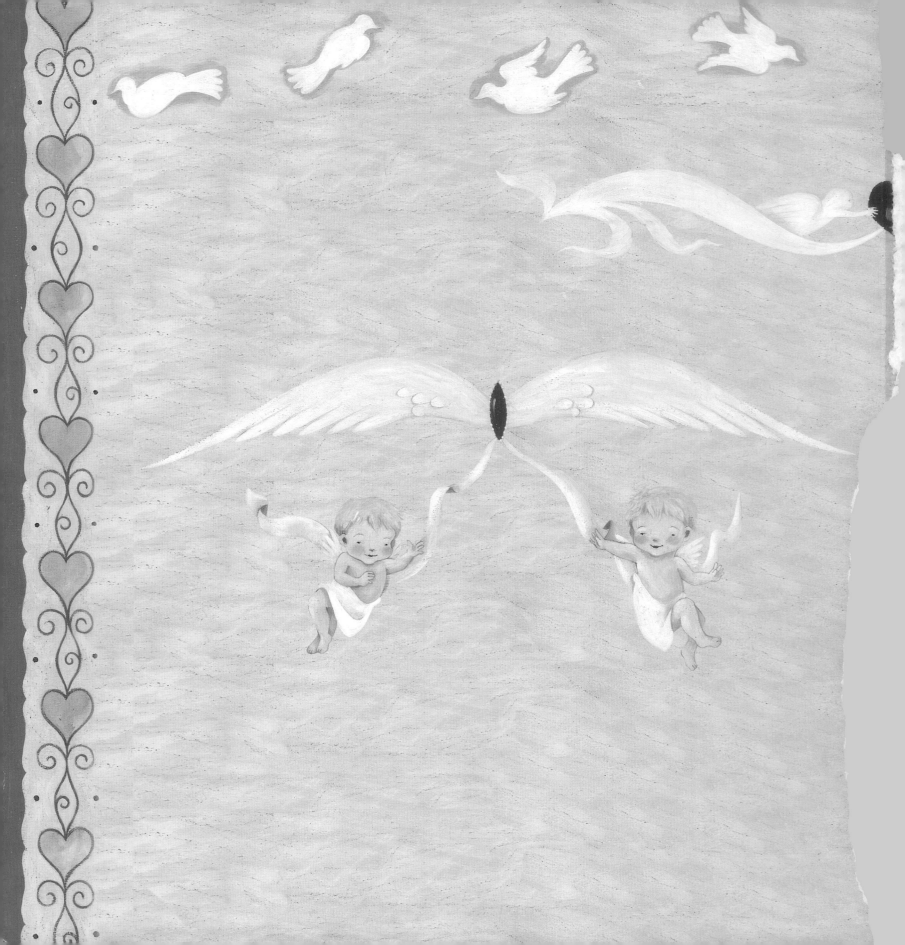